WIKKEDWILLISSAGA

John Lorne Campbell

WIKKEDWILLISSAGA
The Nine Lives of Wicked William

Illustrated by Laura Barrett
Biography of John Lorne Campbell
by Hugh Cheape

WikkedWillisSaga
first published 2015
by Grace Note Publications C.I.C.
Grange of Locherlour,
Ochtertyre, PH7 4JS, Scotland
books@gracenotereading.co.uk
www.gracenotepublications.co.uk

ISBN 978-1-907676-63-5

A catalogue record for this book is available from the British Library

Grace Note Publications thanks Magda Sagarzazu for
initiating this project drawing on the archives of
John Lorne Campbell and Margaret Fay Shaw

Grace Note Publications thanks Ian MacDonald,
Magda Sagarzazu and Hugh Cheape, Sabhal Mòr Ostaig,
for their help in the creation of this book

With thanks to The National Trust for Scotland, which
cares for the John Lorne Campbell and Margaret Fay Shaw
Archives in the Isle of Canna

the National Trust for Scotland
Urras Nàiseanta na h-Alba
a place for everyone   àite don h-uile duine

Faodaidh cat sealltainn air rìgh

CONTENTS

WIKKEDWILLISSAGA

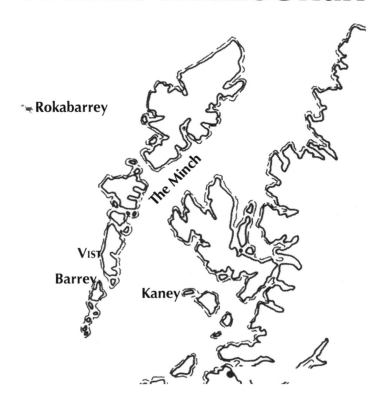

Rokabarrey

The Minch

Vist

Barrey

Kaney

SOUTH VIST

The Beginning

THERE was a cat called Thomas the Black, the kitten of Silky, kitten of Muirchertach. He was a pure-bred Persian, but his wife was baseborn. He belonged to a grocer who lived on Vist in the Southern Isles, and was famous for deeds of valour and skill in the hunt.

One time Thomas the Black and his wife Lissak had a family of five kittens. Their names were Stony, Flann, William, Greta and Poosak. Flann and Greta were drowned in a sack in a loch by Marsaili Nighean Dunnchaidh the wife of the grocer. William was meant to have been drowned, but when the grocer's wife had come to look for the condemned kittens, William had managed to hide in a rubber seaboot beneath the counter of the grocer's shop.

"That is the first of your nine lives," said an old she-cat called Maiseag who was sitting on top of the counter gnawing a piece of ham, and who was famous for wisdom and known to be foresighted. "You will live many years and have many fights, but beware of the day when you lose the last of your four eye-teeth. A cross-eyed cat may yet be your end if you do not then tread warily."

Willi was young and reckless and so lived much in the moment; he did not give much attention to Maseag's warning. Indeed, having succeeded in cheating the sack, his thoughts were now given to the prospects of securing his late brother's and sister's share of the dinner. He also speculated on the time it would take him to grow big enough to be able to jump on the counter and snatch bacon or cheese when the grocer's back was turned. Competition was keen and a young cat needed to look out for himself.

The tread of the grocer returning from the Post Office was heard. Maiseag jumped down from the counter like a flash in spite of all her age and learning. As she jumped, she knocked off a box of kippers. The box fell on the floor and split open; some kippers fell out.

"I will be blamed for this," said William, "but it is better to hang with a full belly," so he grabbed a kipper and retreated behind a box of tangerines, growling a warning to any competitors that might be around. His growling, however, betrayed him to the enraged grocer, who pulled out the box of tangerines to discover William with his booty.

"Get out of here," he shouted angrily, "you have started to steal before even earning your keep." William did not stay around to argue with him. He made off for the Pier with what remained of his herring. At the Pier many an outlawed cat was able to exist by intercepting shipments and levying tolls on foodstuffs that were carelessly stowed. When the fishermen happened to land a catch of herring for export on a merchant vessel, enough might be had to keep a cat alive for a fortnight. There were even stories told of a very fierce cat who more than once had encountered and vanquished live lobsters in boxes on the Pier; but it was generally accepted by Christian cats that this cat was rather a figure of mythology than of true history.

Willi at the Pier

So William went down to the Pier, and the grocer passes out of our story, as do William's parents. He was now on his own and would need to depend on his cunning and muscles.

The door of a large shed was open and thither William directed his footsteps without waiting to look behind him or to the side. But as he ran through the door a big grey cat ambled forward to meet him. Willi slowed down.

"I am called Grim," said the grey cat, "and you are going to give me that herring."

"No cat ever got anything from me but a scratched nose and bitten ears," said William boldly, although the truth was that he had never fought with anyone except his own brothers and young cousins, so that he did not feel so bold as his words.

"Har-r-r-r-r," said Grim as he clouted Willi. Willi dropped the kipper and Grim grabbed it. As he grabbed it Willi gave him a box on the ear, and then scampered out of reach.

"It is reckless to box Grim," growled the grey cat, as he chewed the kipper (what was left of it); "many have paid with their lives for less," he added.

Grim's Slaying

ILLI watched Grim, growlingly devouring the kipper, from the top of a box of tea that was just beyond Grim's spring. He was nervous inwardly but did not let it show. Grim finished the kipper and then he got up and stretched himself and tried out his claws.

"That box shall now be avenged," growled Grim Greycat.

"Try to avenge it," said William.

Grim sprang at Willi, who jumped down behind the box. Grim came after him and chased him round the box three times. The fourth time Willi darted out and dived for shelter into a coil of rope. Grim took hold of the rope at one end and started uncoiling it off Willi. Willi took hold of the rope, and when he felt Grim had it tight he let it go. Grim fell over backwards and slid along the floor so that his head struck a barrel of flour and the barrel burst, burying Grim under flour and stunning him; but Willi's hind leg was caught fast in a coil of the rope and he could not free himself. He was in this predicament, that if he could not get free of the rope before Grim recovered his senses and got the flour out of his eyes, he would meet his doom at Grim's claws.

There was a box of lobsters in the shed and Willi was able to thrust a coil of the rope into the box and between the claws of a lobster and so free himself. At the same time there was a heaving in the flour and Grim arose dustily and looked about him.

The top of the barrel was a circular piece of wood and this Grim took and flung at Willi so that if it had hit him it would have cut him in two; but Willi jumped and the barrel top passed beneath his feet and crashed into an empty whisky bottle that was standing beside the wall.

Willi took the head and neck of the bottle and hurled it at Grim and struck his right ear off. Then he took to his heels and made out of the shed as fast as he could, for Grim looked very angry and was about to corner him.

Grim pursued Willi on to the Pier.

There was a barrel of paraffin on the Pier, and Willi jumped on to the top of the barrel, but he missed the top and only caught the edge. The barrel fell over backwards and knocked Grim into the water, where he drowned miserably, for it was low tide and he could neither catch the piles of the Pier nor swim. On the next day his body was found on an islet and this has been called Grimsey, i.e. Grim's Island, from that time forth.

Willi Escapes from the Pier

THERE was a man called Angus-Ian. He had a small fishing boat which was often at the Pier. The day after Grim's slaying his boat was at the Pier, but he was in the Bar, drinking.

Now the blood feud was on foot and Grim's brothers and uncles were seeking to slay Willi without thought of accepting atonement. Willi was hiding in a pile of draining tiles on the Pier. He could not go to find help without exposing himself to the danger of attack, and his master the grocer had already outlawed him. Inside the shed two of Grim's brothers were searching for him, and a third was looking for him under the Pier, on the crossbeams, while Grim's uncle and another brother were watching the paths that led away from the Pier.

A woman came down from the grocer's shop with a large basket. She laid down the basket beside the pile of tiles on the Pier while she went to look for Angus-Ian to take her over the bay. Willi crept out of the tile-pile and into the basket, which was covered with thick brown paper and contained some crockery wrapped up in straw. He had hardly done this when Grim's brothers came out of the shed and started going through the draining tiles.

The woman and Angus-Ian came down to the Pier and then the woman lifted up her basket to get into the boat. Just before, Grim's brothers had scented something of Willi in the basket and were preparing to attack him. "Clear off," said the woman of the basket, and chased Grim's brothers away.

"That may be the second of my nine lives," said William, "but the future cannot be worse," and he lay down in the basket, which was handed aboard to Angus-Ian. The boat then left the Pier and made off for the other side of the bay, where Grim's relations could hardly be expected to follow.

The woman was called Mairi-Anndra and half way over the bay she lifted the paper to look at the crockery she had just bought. Willi sat up and blinked at her.

"A peashak," said she, "a half-Persian too. That'll be the grocer's kitten. Well, he'll not miss it. I can do with a cat in the house." So she took Willi home in the basket and gave him some scone and milk for supper. "Now catch mousies," she told him. Willi purred and fell asleep by the fire.

SUDHRLOCHBADHASTILL

Willi and Martin Angusruascat

THERE was a cat called Martin Angusruascat. He was a big tom tabby and very fierce and proud. It was said of him that he had even vanquished several other cats in the "ordeal by combat."[1] He was acknowledged the head amongst the cats of Sudhrlochbadhastill and all of them feared him greatly.

It was not long before Martin Angusruascat heard that a new young tomcat had come to the house of Mairi-Anndra.

"They say he slew Grim," said one of Martin's followers.

"What was Grim to me," replied Martin: "even if he slew him fairly (which I doubt), I shall still make catsmeat of this truant upstart," and he spat at the dresser and put out a candle. " Just wait till I get my claws on him."

---

[1] A special form of duelling whereby two cats who had become mortal enemies would tie their tails together and fight to the death. No escape was possible, of course. ED.

Willi was living at Mairi-Anndrasstadhir. He had settled down, and had been given a wife called Fluffl. Fluffl was handsome, but vain and greedy. Willi and she did not hit it off though he cared well enough for their kittens, Maolsk and Finnla Williskitten. One evening Willi was out hunting rabbits and Fluffl was sitting dozing by the stove. Mairi-Anndra was asleep in the back room. Martin Angusruascat came looking for William and trouble. He pushed his way in through the cathole in the door, walked into the kitchen, and collected a booty of oatcakes and butter. When Fluffl waked up he started to beguile her, telling her she was beautiful and wise. "And," said he, "you would be better off with me than with William."

"I belong to the braver," said she; "fight it out together."

Now William was coming home with a young rabbit he had caught, and Martin Angusruascat was waiting for him behind the cathole in the door with an axe, waiting to take the head from his shoulders the moment he put it inside. William reached the cathole and he flung in the young rabbit. It was dark and Martin Angusruascat swung his axe and cut the young rabbit in half thinking his blow was falling on William's neck.

"That was an ill deed you thought of," said William, "but you will pay for it," and he dealt him a blow on the head that knocked him over; but Martin Angusruascat came back at him and hit Willi head over heels so that he was flung out of the door on to the midden. Then Willi threw a stone at Martin, but it missed him and hit Fluffl, who was watching the combat, and Fluffl screamed. "Those cats," said Mairi-Anndra, and she got up and reached for a broomstick, and then clouted Martin Angusruascat out of the door, so that he was hurled past Willi; but Martin spat at him in passing and swore to be avenged.

Martin Angusruascat's Slaying

NOT LONG after, it was in the evening and Willi was coming home over the hill with a booty of blackbirds' eggs and he was crossing a peat moor when Martin Angusruascat stepped out from behind a pile of peat and confronted him.

"Now we must fight it out to the bitter end, who shall be bosscat in Sudhrlochbadhastill, you or I," said Martin.

"I am willing," said Willi, and he spat on his paws.

Willi advanced half sideways towards Martin, and aimed a blow at his ear; but Martin jumped in the air and the blow was spent on nothing. Then Martin smote Willi on the head with a downward blow so that his head was smitten into the mud and stuck there, but Willi stretched out his right paw and pulled Martin's feet from under him and sent him rolling into a puddle. Then he pulled his own head out of the mud. Martin scrambled out of the puddle and flung himself on Willi and tried to bite his throat, but Willi's thick fur got in the way of his teeth and he got nothing but fur. Willi rolled under Martin and raked Martin's belly with his hind claws, but Martin bit through one of Willi's ears.

Then they set on each other, and in their struggle they pounded the rocks into mud and the mud into rocks, and where their blows fell on the hillside there gushed forth springs of clear fresh water; when they sank least in the peat bog 'twas to their knees and where they sank most in the peat bog they went down to their eyes; but at the last William remembered that he was near to his foes and far from his friends, so he collected himself for one final effort and succeeded in hurling Martin Angusruascat into a deep peat tarn. Martin could not swim, and Willi cast peats into the tarn until the surface of the water was covered, so that there was no way for Martin to get out of the water. Then he sang this song:

Ill fared the tabby lean and tattered
'Gainst Wicked William in wounding battle:
Though thick thy skull, my skin was thicker –
Hair alone didst thou bite – a bitter dinner.

William fared home to Taigh-Mairi-Anndra, and he was covered with mud from head to tail, as well as with the scars of battle; so that at first his own wife Fluffl did not recognise him. They washed him and dressed his wounds, and the fame he gained from Martin Angusruascat's slaying was very great. But Willi reflected that when Martin's axe had divided the young rabbit instead of severing his head, it might very well have been the third of his nine lives.

Willi Fares to Barrey

Now WILLI waxed fierce and proud, and was greatly feared and respected; he led many forays and

collected much booty from kitchens, larders and rubbish heaps. But as the saying goes, "There is no success but envy follows," so other jealous and desperate cats (the friends and relations of Martin Angusruascat and Grim) met together and plotted to slay him by force of overpowering numbers. Willi was still an outlaw from the grocer's outlawing, though Taigh-Mairi-Anndra was a good sanctuary for him. Though many feared him he had not the support of blood-relations in the district, for his son, Finnla Williskitten, had gone on a viking expedition to Mikkiley south of Barrey and had settled there.

Now Fluffl, Willi's wife, died of a surfeit of condensed cream when Mairi-Anndra had spilt a tin on the floor; but those evil cats, the friends and followers of Angusruascat and Grim, put it about assiduously that Willi had poisoned her, as it was known that the two of them did not agree well together. This story gained credence amongst the relations of Fluffl and they too joined with the relations of Martin and Grim in plotting William's destruction and death.

It was not long after this that Mairi-Anndra was over at the Pier to shop. Now Maiseag the spaecat who was foresighted had heard of the conspiracies of the friends of Grim and knew the great danger Willi was running in Sudhrlochbadhistill. So she took this chance to send Willi a warning in Mairi-Anndra's shopping basket. It was in verse:

Grim's and Fluffl's friends, with Martin's,
Seek to slay thee, so beware:
Fare to Barrey, fearless viking –
No cat can betray thee there.

Maiseag knew that Willi would be sure to inspect Mairi-Anndra's groceries, and so would be sure to find the warning. So it happened. Willi was loath to go, but he respected Maiseag's foresight. He had powerful friends amongst the humans of Barrey and he knew that if he fared there on a viking expedition no cat would dare to reproach him with cowardice or having fled there for shelter and safety.

So it turned out. Willi bade farewell to Mairi-Anndra circumspectly, prepared for his expedition and set sail with a favouring wind and came to harbour at Nordhrvagr in the island of Barrey. He took up his dwelling with the human Mairead Ni Sheathaich, whom he had once met in Vist.

BARREY

Willi's Adventures in Barrey

HERE was a cat called Kiteen Donalscat, who lived in a house not far from Willi's dwelling at Nordhrvagr; she had kittens by Willi, who used to visit her after dark. When the kittens were growing up, Willi said, "One shall come with me and I shall father him." "Not so," said Kiteen, "to every cow her calf, to every she-cat her kittens," and she spat at Willi and boxed his ear. Willi did not wait to argue but grabbed his kitten and so out of the window with it between his teeth.

Kiteen raised such a howl that the humans in the house were awakened, and a shower of missiles and weapons descended on Willi, and oaths were heard. A shoe struck Willi and caused him to slip and drop the kitten; the shower became so intense no cat could have faced it and Willi ran for home. That was the only time that Willi ran and it was before men and not before cats. He counted it the fourth of his lives lost for the great danger he had been in from shoes, stones and old bottles. The kitten was never seen again and Kiteen Donalscat did not ever forgive Willi.

It was about this time that the tabby Wimpikitten was taken into the household of Mairead Ni Sheathaich. Willi took to him at first and reared him, but after Wimpikitten grew up there came a great coldness between them and finally a battle, after which Wimpi left the household and went to live elsewhere.

It was while Mairead Ni Sheathaich and her husband were on a visit to Greenland that Willi was taken into the household of the Bishop of Nordhrvagr, and given a wife called Scot; but this turned out ill, as Willi had a quarrel with Slate, Scot's brother, over a mutton bone, and would have killed Slate but for the Bishop's intervention. Willi was thereafter in such danger from the wrath of the Bishop that he deemed a fifth life must be gone, and took refuge in the house of Rurik Krkl; but much the same thing happened to him here. When Mairead Ni Sheathaich returned from Greenland Willi was glad to get back to her home.

Now Willi was feared and respected throughout the north of Barrey, and committed many forays and collected much booty; but he avoided such catslaughters as might have brought on dangerous bloodfeuds and conspiracies against him. His worst foes were the cats in the households of the Bishop and Rurik. So it fared with Willi until the famous slaying of Duncan Jonsskitten, which must now be related.

Willi and Duncan Jonsskitten

THERE was a cat called Duncan Jonsskitten; he lived in the palace of a great and famous skaldess called Anna Jonsdottir. Duncan was strong and a mighty fighter; at the south end of Barrey all cats held him in fear. His colour was tabby and white, his ears were battered and his claws were long. Duncan was a great viking;

he had fared as far as Bjarnarey to the south and Eiriksey to the north and had done great deeds of valour and gained enormous booty.

One day there came tales of Willi's doings at Nordhrvagr. "Let us sail there," said Duncan to his henchcats; "if this Willi has booty, it will be ours," and so they set sail in his galley which was called *Sharksword*, and with a following wind sailed northward for Hellisay point, then in westwards past Flatey and so into the harbour of Nordhrvagr, which is long, winding and narrow.

Now Willi had the fishing of salmon in Nordhrvagr through the strength of his claws though not by written law, and that day he had out his salmon net stretched across from one side of the harbour to the other. He was waiting on a rock above one end of the net watching to see the salmon strike the net as they ran up the bay to enter the river that runs into the top of the bay. Laxa is the name of that river, that is, salmon stream.

Duncan and his henchcats came into the bay on the galley *Sharksword* with sail set and twelve at the oars, so their speed was great.

Willi arose on the rock and motioned and shouted to them to stop outside in the bay below his salmon net, but never a sign from *Sharksword* that anything had been seen or heard. The ship sailed into the bay at speed with Duncan at the helm and cut through the net. As they cut it, all caterwauled with laughter. Then they slowed down to put out a cat on the side of the bay opposite Willi to pull in that half of the net so that they should have it and the salmon in it, and Duncan Jonskitten sang:

> Wicked Willi, weak as water,
> Thin the fare thou'lt find to-day.
> Fetch a fishhook, Wicked Willi,
> Tie it to your tattered tail,
> Soak it in the swirling seawaves –
> Sure, you'll catch a shark or whale.

Willi had his fish-spear with him and he flung it at Duncan. Duncan avoided it, but it went past him and into the side of *Sharksword*, making a hole below the water line. Duncan then ordered part of his cats to pull for an inlet in the shore where they might patch the hole, and the other part to let fly a volley of arrows at Willi; but Willi was off for help from his friends and the arrows all fell behind him.

Willi Attacks Duncan

THERE were many cats around Nordhrvagr who feared Willi but hated Duncan Jonsskitten more. Willi soon collected his own friends and some of these other cats and launched his own galley *Eelnose* in the hope of catching Duncan Jonsskitten and his cats before they had mended the hole in the bottom of *Sharksword* made by Willi's fish spear; and meanwhile another band of Willi's henchcats were sent overland around the bay to the little promontory on which *Sharksword* had been pulled ashore to attack Duncan Jonsskitten's band in the rear from the land, while Willi and the cats on board *Eelnose* attacked them from the sea. Thus it was hoped to cut off Duncan Jonsskitten and his friends from all sides and destroy them all without mercy.

The friends of Willi were now on the promontory where *Sharksword* was beached, and Duncan Jonsskitten and his cats worked desperately to patch the keel of *Sharksword* so that they could put to sea and would not have to fight on the beach where they would be at a disadvantage. They were just finishing this work when the band of Willi's friends appeared above them on the hillock that overlooked the beach, and poured down on them such a shower of weapons, javelins, spears, rotten eggs, stink bombs, jam jars, stones, plates, dishes and old boots and shoes that no band of cats, however brave, could have withstood it. Duncan Jonsskitten and his crew pushed *Sharksword* down the beach and into the sea and aboard with them, but they were in such a hurry that they had to leave five or six cats ashore who were obliged to face the friends of Willi, led by his old friend Wimpi, without hope of assistance, for Willi himself in *Eelnose* was bearing down on *Sharksword* all ready for battle.

Now Duncan Jonaskitten, as soon as *Sharksword* had been beached, had despatched a cat with messages to the cats and followers of the Bishop of Nordhrvagr and Rurik Krkl and the friends of Kiteen Donalscat, all of whom hated Willi, asking them to come quickly, as now there would be a chance to deal with the tyrant of Nordhrvagr; and he said many other ill words of Willi, seeking to stir up the resentment that is never lacking in cats that have been crossed in love or forestalled on the rubbish heap, so that many such cats collected, for this messenger had the luck to avoid the party led by Wimpi that went round Nordhrvagr to attack Duncan Jonsskitten on the beach from the land.

Slate Slatesson, cat of the Bishop of Nordhrvagr, led this band of evil-minded cats back towards the very same promontory where Wimpi and his cats were now just about to cast their missiles at Duncan Jonsskitten and his crew.

About this time it happened through sheer chance that Grim Greycatskitten from Loch Badhistill had fared south to Barrey on a viking expedition, and was approaching Nordhrvagr; while Finnla Willisson and his friends had left Mikkeley in their galley to pay a visit to Willi at Nordhrvagr, for Finnla had not seen Willi his father since the day that he (Finnla) had sailed from Loch Badhistill to Mikkeley, and had settled there. He wished to consult with Willi about a joint viking expedition against the island of Eiriksey. Both Grimskitten and Finnla approached Nordhrvagr about the same time, as will be seen from this story.

The Battle of Nordhrvagr

Now we must turn to the doings of Willi and his crew who were bearing down on the *Sharksword* in their galley *Eelnose* ready to attack Duncan and his benchcats. Willi had his sword Tigrtallon with him, and his cats were in full battle dress.

Willi hailed Duncan. "Miserable miaouler, you hoped for booty, but you will be lucky to

escape with the last of your nine lives." "You will do well to keep the last of yours," shouted Duncan, and with that the battle started. There was a shower of weapons from both galleys as they came alongside one another and were made fast together side by side. Then the crew of each sought to jump aboard the other and cut down their opponents or fling them into the sea. The air was thick with flying fur and resounded with the cries of battle.

Willi took his good sword Tigrtallon, which was so sharp it could cut a straw borne by a summer breeze on the top of the sea, or a gossamer falling through the air; its hilt was studded with jewels that sparkled in the sunshine like fireworks, and the flash from its blade was as dazzling as lightning. With this sword he could cut down nine cats on his right hand and nine cats on his left and find it ready again for the next blow; where the throng against him was thickest, 'twould be scattered furthest; and when 'twas scattered furthest, 'twas soonest slaughtered. And although a cat had the tongues of twenty poets in his head and all of them making rhymes day and night long they would not suffice to tell all the deeds of valour and heroism, slaughter and slaying that were done with this wonderful weapon.

Willi jumped aboard *Sharksword* and made straight for Duncan Jonsskitten, who was doing great execution amongst the followers of Willi. He made a sweep at Duncan with Tigrtallon but Duncan stooped and the sword passed over his head. It struck the mast of *Sharksword* and severed it completely. The mast toppled over backwards and laid Duncan and Willi both senseless.

Now while the other cats aboard *Sharksword* and *Eelnose* were continuing their battle, the six brave cats left behind on the Rudha Mor when *Sharksword* was launched in a hurry were defending themselves valiantly against the overwhelming numbers of Wimpi's band, but were being pressed into the water, wounded and drowning, by the sheer weight of numbers and missiles. Meanwhile Slate Slatesson and his cats were marching down the promontory and attacked Wimpi's band itself from the rear, so that the battle raged still more fiercely, and Wimpi himself was now outnumbered.

And while the battle raged ashore and on the sea, the galley of Grimskitten from Loch Badhistill entered the bay. Grimskitten sees the flag of Willi flying from the mast of *Eelnose*, and *Sharksword* dismasted. "That is the galley of Willi Thomasson," said Grimskitten to his crew, "and now I shall avenge my father the Greycat."

He drew alongside *Eelnose* and saw sure enough that it was Willi in the battle.

Willi Slays Duncan Jonsskitten – Finnla Willison Helps Willi but Is Slain

ow Willi and his cats are in very great straits between two hostile galleys and outnumbered by two to one. Willi and Duncan came to their senses about the same moment. Willi was about to attack Duncan again, but the cries of his crew made him turn first against Grim Grimskitten's cats. But Duncan pressed against Willi from the rear, and Willi was forced to turn and fight him. Duncan strikes at him with his sword and pierces Willi's foot. Willi struck at Duncan with his sword Tigrtallon, but missed him. The sword, however, cut through the thwart on which Duncan was standing and severed it completely, dropping Duncan into the bilges or the *Sharksword*. Before he could climb out of the bilge, Willi struck off his head. So perished Duncan Jonsskitten. He was a fierce and valiant cat, but hard, and the fame of his slaying was very great. His death struck sorrow into the hearts of his crew, and their efforts became weak, but the crew of Grimskitten pressed Willi's cats harder than ever.

About this time Finnla Willison entered the bay, and heard the shouting and cries of battle. "My father will be there," he said, "let us hasten." He found Willi between the galleys of Grimskitten and Duncan as has been related. He pulled alongside Grimskitten's galley and attacked it. He sought out Grimskitten, and made as to strike him with his sword, but when Grimskitten crouched away from the sword Finnla flung his spear at him with his left hand. (He had lost his shield.) The spear entered Grimskitten's throat and it killed him. Just then four of Grimskitten's cats struck Finnla down from behind, so that he too died; but these four cats Willi destroyed with one blow from Tigrtallon.

Now Duncan and Grimskitten were slain, but Finnla is dead, and all the shores of Nordhrvagr were held by the followers of Slate Slatesson the Bishop's cat, except the promontory where the remnants of Wimpi's band were in their turn hard-pressed by overwhelming numbers.

Then spoke one of Willi's crew, saying: "I can see nothing for it but to leave Nordhrvagr and seek a haven elsewhere, for we cannot land here without all being killed; let us save whom we can of Wimpi's band, and then take to the sea."

Willi said: "It is no honour to be driven from the field of battle."

"Honour is saved," said another of the crew. "You have slain Duncan Jonsskitten and our kitten Finnla has been avenged. Let Duncan's friends seek us again if they wish vengeance. We will face them anywhere."

So it was decided, and so it was done. They took Wimpi and the survivors of his band from the short of the point, and away to the open sea, but Willi and Slate hurled curses at each other at parting.

The battle of Nordhrvagr was famous for many a day after this, and it was said that no such slaughter was ever known before or after in battles of cats, so that the waters of the bay were red for weeks after, like wine; but

I (Frukjan) think this second statement is an exaggeration.

CROSSING THE MINCH

How Willi Sailed to Kaney

ILLI and Wimpi and their henchcats rowed their galley out of Nordhrvagr followed by the curses and missiles of Slate Slatesson and the hostile cats of Nordhrvagr. When they got to the mouth of the bay they hoisted sail. The wind, which had earlier been in the south, had shifted to the south-west. They sailed east of the point of Hellisey where the cave (Hellir) is, and then tried to make the sound that is between the islands of Hellisey and Gioghey; but the wind freshened against them in the entrance of the sound and they were unable to enter it either with sail or with oars. Then they tried to make for the east side of Eiriksey where they would have shelter from the wind which now blew from the west, but they could not hold their course across the Barreyjarsund owing to the strength of the wind and the currents and the great size of the waves. There was nothing for it but to turn eastwards and run before the wind for Kaney or Colla. Willi chose to steer from Kaney because there was a haven, but Colla had neither haven nor shelter.

They ran before the wind with the sails fully reefed and at that the strength of the wind was bending the mast and threatening to tear the canvas of the sail and to break asunder the ropes. The galley *Eelnose* had a mast of silver, a rudder of gold carefully engraved with lucky runes and secret oghams, and ropes made of thousands of strands of the finest spun silk; her planks were of bog oak, her thwarts of hazel, and her sails of bog-cotton spun and woven. But for the skill of the hands that wove her sails and built her keel and fashioned her gear, and the virtue of the runes and oghams that had been skilfully and carefully carved on her rudder and prow, it would have gone ill with her in the terrible storm that was now blowing up. Her prow was carved in the shape of a conger-eel's head, from which her name, that is, *Eelnose*.

Loudly the wind shrieked and the waves rose as high as mountains, while thunder deafened the air and lightning lit up the skies blinding all who beheld it. Foam and spray rose from the crest of the waves to the skies and mingled with the hail and rain that fell from the lowering clouds; ghostly mists mingled with the swirling snow that again and again encircled the sailors, while from distant shores the crash of the breakers re-echoed the booming of the thunder. Where the crest of the waves was highest, it rose to the skies; and where the trough of the waves was lowest, it descended to the sea bed, so that angel fish, lampreys, giant skates and spider crabs, prawns and electric eels and other horrible monsters of the deep were often brought to the surface of the water. Willi was steering *Eelnose* and it needed all his skill and daring to keep her from becoming engulfed in the inferno of waters.

There was a momentary lull and suddenly they saw a black shape rising out of the water. Willi tried to avoid it but it came rapidly towards them. The monster, for so it was, had a single huge red eye in the middle of its forehead that darted glancing hither and thither more quickly than a star will twinkle on

a frosty winter night. Blue flames issued from its nostrils at each exhalation of its breath. It had a forked tongue, and teeth in its jaws of which the smallest would have served for a dagger and the greatest for a doorpost. It had four short legs with feet like a frog's hands and a long tail. Try as he could, Willi could not avoid it. It soon caught up with the boat and put a forefoot on the gunwale, breathing flames all over the deck. If the wind and rain had not been so heavy *Eelnose* might well have caught fire from this pestilent breath.

Willi was at a loss, as he had stowed his good sword Tigrtallon out of reach while steering the galley. The rest of the crew were stricken with terror.

"Who are you?" said Willi.

"I am the Muilgheartach Mhaol Bhuidhe, Mial Mhor a' Chuain, the bald yellow Mullarty monster of the Minch, first cousin to Midhgardhsorm the serpent that encircles the world. None can cross the seas here without paying me tribute."

"What is the tribute?"

"The tribute is this: four-fifths of your

goods and two-thirds of your cats to make fur coats for my seals."

"The first you might have but the second never."

"Then I will take everything."

The monster placed its other foreleg on the stern of the galley, threatening to sink it, and opened wide its mouth as if to swallow Willi. The stern anchor was beside Willi and he took it and flung it into the maw of the monster. Then, while the monster was choking over the anchor, he took his sword Tigrtallon which Wimpi had put into his hand furtively and with one blow struck out the monster's eye and with another severed both her forefeet, so that she fell back into the sea and perished miserably. Great was the joy of the rest of the crew at their deliverance from such a dire danger; but they agreed to share the knowledge of the deed with few, for fear that some cats might not believe them. This is how I, Frukjan, have heard the story related by ancient and learned cats well skilled in tradition, so I set it down here as I have heard it myself, neither adding to or taking from it anything, so that those who come after me may best judge for themselves, according to their own disposition and experience. It is said indeed that one of the monster's teeth broke off and was left sticking in the gunwale and was afterwards kept by the descendants of Willi as a remembrance of his valour in the slaying of the Mullarty; but I, Frukjan, have not seen this tooth.

Willi and his crew sailed on past fearful caverns and towering cliffs and sheer rocks and eventually found a passage through a number of foam-clad skerries into a channel through which they passed into Kaneyjarhafn where they were sheltered from the terrible wind and fierce seas outside. When they had reached Kaney and had gone ashore, they laid their hands on the gunwale of their galley *Eelnose* and drew her seven times her own length up on to the green grass, where neither wind could shift her nor sun scorch her nor the impudent stray cats of the city reach her to make a mock of her. They went ahead until they reached the habitations of humans, and the humans of Kaney were good to them.

This then had been the career of Willi up till the time that he landed in Kaney. He had lost one life in his encounter with Grim and another in his fight with Martin Angsruascat at Loch Badhistill, not to speak of a third when the grocer nearly drowned him as a kitten in the loch. A fourth life was gone when he barely escaped from the enraged friends of Kiteen Donalscat at Nordhrvagr, and a fifth in his fearful battle with Duncan Jonsskitten and his friends there. A sixth life was gone when he survived the terrible tempest and the gruesome monster, the bald yellow Mullarty, on his voyage from Barrey to Kaney. He had now three lives left and was at the height of his strength and his fame when he landed on Kaney with his crew and his good galley *Eelnose* after leaving the battle at Nordhrvagr.

LIFE IN KANEY

Willi Finds Quarters on Kaney

A T the time that Willi and Wimpi and their cats arrived at Kaney in the galley *Eelnose*, the King of the cats of Kaney was Pietr Pietskitten who lived at a place called the Square. He was a big dark grey tabby and very fierce, and the cats of Kaney all acknowledged his sway. There was a race of greycats of Kaney related to Grim; their leader was called Gorry Greycat. These were the cats that lived around the houses of humans on Kaney; but there was also a race of berserk cats of very great size and fierceness who dwelt in the hills and rocks of Kaney and lived by the chase, for Kaney abounded in rabbits and blackbirds and game of all kinds. These cats feared nobody and only nominally acknowledged the authority of King Pietr; but as they were always divided by feuds and quarrels between themselves, they were not such a menace to the security of his kingdom as they might have been.

It must be related that after they had landed in Kaney, Willi and Wimpi disagreed about the division of the booty they had brought over from Nordhrvagr, and finally they and their bands separated after casting lots for certain of the goods, and went their ways to different human habitations where they took up their abodes and did not see each other thereafter. There would certainly have been fighting over the division of this booty but for the fact that enough sense prevailed for them not to weaken their numbers in face of the Kaney cats who might otherside have taken advantage of them to steal all the booty themselves. Willi made his way to the house of Mairead Ni Sheathaich, who now lived on Kaney; Wimpi went to another house and now passes out of this story.

Great was the envy and the displeasure of the cats of Kaney when they saw the honoured and secured positions that were given to Willi and Wimpi; but the fame of each was well known and none dared directly to attack them. Willi had small trouble to slay Gorry Greycat and disperse his followers. He sent an embassy to King Pietr with gifts and good wishes, but as an equal and not as a vassal. Pietr would have spurned the gifts, but his queen was greedy and would not let them go. He brooded on the presence of Willi, for something told him that his kingdom might be in danger.

So it was one morning that when King Pietr went to the dairy he found the cream dish empty and tongue marks on the butter. The padlock on the door had been filed through and was lying in the mud.

Willi and Pietr, King of the Cats of Kaney

GREAT was the wrath of King Pietr when he found the lock of the dairy broken and the cream and butter stolen. He called together his courtiers and his followers to inquire if anyone had seen or heard the thief.

"Perhaps it was rats," said one of them.

"No rat could jump on the dairy table," said Pietr.

"Then it was Willi from Barrey, whom cats call Wicked Willi Thomasskitten," said another.

"Who will drive him from Kaney?" said Pietr; but there did not seem to be anybody ready to come forward.

"Perhaps we could hide behind a wall and cut him down in the darkness?"

"Or lie in wait on the cliff above the road and roll stones down on his head?"

"Or push him off the Pier, or shoot arrows into his bedroom?"

"Not so," said King Pietr, "for if it went well, cats would say that we had slain him by treachery and deceit, and if it went ill, Willi would then gather a band together and try to destroy us," for he feared that Willi might make common cause with the wildcats in the hills.

"What shall we do then?" asked one of the courtiers.

"We shall prepare a trap here for him," said King Pietr, "so that if he comes thieving again, he is fairly taken, and his right paw and ears at least shall be forfeit, if he lose not his life," and the other cats applauded and said it was a good plan.

"How will it be done?" said one.

"I must think awhile," said King Pietr.

Pietr Takes Willi

AFTER King Pietr had spent some hours in reflection, he devised the following scheme. He loosened the boards of the dairy table so that if anyone jumped up on it they would fall and he with them. He put a platter of cream and a dish of butter on the table and a big barrel underneath it. The barrel was half filled with water on top of which he put some bran so that the barrel appeared to hold nothing but bran. Then he arranged a net so that it could be pulled over the top of the barrel by a string that was passed out of the window of the dairy and over into a shed where he and his cats would spend the night in hiding.

Darkness came and, sure enough, before long some cat arrived and tried the dairy door. A new padlock had been put on but it soon yielded to a little filing. The door was then slowly seen to open and a dark figure glided inside. There was the sound of padded feet up-jumping and then an appalling crash and rattle and such swear words as had never before been heard by any cat of them. Pietr pulled the string that should drag the net over the mouth of the barrel, and then ordered his cats to fetch lanterns and enter the dairy and see Willi (or whoever it was) secured.

Willi indeed it was who had gone down to try his fortune at the dairy. When he had made his way in and jumped on the table to get at the cream, it had happened as King Pietr had devised. The boards of the table had given way, letting Willi fall through into the barrel with a crash and a splash; the cream platter had shot up in the air, pouring its contents all over Willi, and the butter had left the plate and had landed on his left ear and eye. It was all he could do to keep from drowning in the barrel, and he was covered with water and bran where he was not plastered with butter and cream. Then he heard the net drawn over his head, and knew his very great danger.

King Pietr's cats entered the dairy with torches and swords and they found Willi in the barrel and they quickly covered the top of the barrel with a sack because they did not dare to trust the net to keep him inside the barrel, but feared that he might tear it and escape. Then they hoisted the barrel on poles and brought it before King Pietr.

"Who will open the barrel," said King Pietr, "so that we may try this miserable marauder and inflict on him a just sentence?" But no cat seemed to be very anxious to come forward to open the barrel.

"Why not try him without opening the barrel?" said one of the courtcats. "After all, if he is condemned to be drowned or burnt, the sentence can be carried out just as well inside the barrel as outside it"; and so it was agreed. A court was at once set up. Two holes were bored in the barrel, one at the foot to let out the water, and one near the top, to allow Willi's pleas to be heard; but when they did hear the kind of things he was saying, King Pietr very quickly ordered his head carpentercat to go and find a bung and shut up this hole, and so it was done and Willi was silenced. They jeered at him, asking him how he liked his bran porridge.

The Trial of Willi and the Slaying of Pietr

Now it must here be said that before Willi had left his dwelling to raid the dairy he had instructed his henchcats that if he were not back at a certain hour they must seek him around the Square. So his Trial was beginning, and this hour was approaching.

The barrel was taken on boards and brought before King Pietr in the hayloft. The prosecution was entrusted to the most learned lawcat of King Pietr's court. There was some discussion as to whether Willi should be allowed to speak for himself or should have his case pled for him by another courtcat. The bung was removed from the barrel so that he could be asked whether he pleaded guilty or not guilty, but all that came out was a volley of oaths and catcalls.

"Replace the bung," said King Pietr. "So that justice may be done to the villain, our junior lawcat may represent him; not that Cicero himself could find anything to say for the scoundrel." So it was done.

The prosecutor spoke and pleaded for the death sentence. He said that Willi had been caught in the act of robbery and *lèse-majesté*; he had slain Gorry Greycat unatoned and had committed murders, robberies and kidnappery in Vist and Barrey. If he were allowed to go free or lightly punished there was no knowing what slayings and rapine he might not commit. King Pietr's kingdom could not be safe with such a reprobate at large, or even locked up alive. They should make an end of him while they had got him.

The defending lawcat could say little except to plead that Willi was a stranger and ignorant of the laws of Kaney, but this plea was brushed aside, for "ignorance is no excuser".

So he was found guilty by the Cat-Thing, and the sentence was that a large anchor should be attached to the barrel by a short rope and all dropped into deep water half a mile from the shore. So an anchor was found and tied tightly to the barrel, and barrel and anchor were lifted on planks and carried down to the beach where King Pietr kept his galley.

They were walking down over the stones on the shore when the cry went up: "Here come the followers of Willi!," and so it was. They had come to seek him at the Square because he had not returned by the hour expected.

Willi's followers saw the party with the barrel and guessed something untoward was happening. They at once made an attack on the cats carrying the barrel, and these dropped the barrel the better to defend themselves. It fell on the stones on the shore, rolled down and burst on a big rock just above the sea water, and Willi was flung out. He was terrible to behold all plastered with bran and cream.

Now Willi sought out King Pietr while the battle raged. He was unarmed but had found a pitchfork and sickle in one of the buildings. At length he met Pietr on the hay loft.

"Now I shall be avenged," said Willi; and Pietr defied him. He flung his pitchfork at Pietr but missed him by a hair's breadth. Pietr struck so hard at Willi with his sword that if he had hit him it would have cloven him in two; but he missed, and the sword's point was buried in the wooden floor of the loft. Before he could draw it out, Willi struck off Pietr's head with his sickle. Then he took the head and flung it down amongst Pietr's followers who were still fighting with Willi's cats below. When they saw the head of King Pietr, panic seized them and they broke and scattered.

After the slaying of King Pietr, Willi's fame was very great, and the cats of Kaney all came and submitted to him, except a few of the wild cats in the mountains. But such an escape as Willi had from the barrel was his seventh life lost.

MORE ADVENTURES IN KANEY

The Giant Glómr

THERE was a giant called Glómr. He had one eye in the middle of his forehead, long matted hair, long fingernails like the talons of a raven, and was several ells taller than any mortal man. He lived in a cave on Kaney called Glómshellir, that is, Glómr's cave. This cave was very big and very dark and in the roof a shaft arose which opened through rocks and stones into the open air .

In this shaft Glómr had hung by an iron chain a huge cauldron in which he stewed flesh of all kinds over a fire made of driftwood. He was voracious and not particular about the nature of his victims. His apparel was a cloak of catskins, his favourite weapon was a huge spiked club. He was ferocious in appearance and nature. Many a cat, it was said, had disappeared into Glómshellir, never to be seen again. Even humans feared him greatly and avoided the neighbourhood of Glómshellir entirely.

Willi Enters Glómshellir

ONE DAY Willi was out hunting on the mountains and ravines of Kaney but no game had fallen to his claws. He had become separated from his henchcats and was tired and wet and hungry. He smelt the smell of flesh cooking, and seeking it came to the cave, that is, Glómshellir, where Glómr lived and kept his cauldron.

Willi had heard tales of the ferocity of Glómr and dangers of Glómshellir but pride as well as hunger made him follow the smell into the cave, believing that if Glómr were there he could still escape him and if he were not a good dinner would reward his boldness. Although the cave was dark as the midwinter night and half filled with smoke and damp with dropping water, and its floor strewed with the bones of cats, rabbits, sheep, oxen and other creatures, Willi made his way forward until he came to the cauldron. Then he stood up on his hind legs and reached down into the cauldron and hooked out a piece of goatsmeat, which he started to eat on the floor.

He was busy at this work when he heard the earth shake and the heavens resound with the coming of Glómr; the air in the cave grew dark and cold, the crying of gulls and ravens without was hushed, and a shadow fell across the mouth of Glómshellir as Glómr entered the cave, closing its mouth with a mighty boulder. He was carrying his mighty club and clothed in catskins, and at once perceived Willi eating his goatsmeat on the floor by the fireside.

The Slaying of Glómr

WHEN Glómr saw Willi eating the dinner that was being prepared for himself, he set the end of his club on the ground and leaned on it, while pondering upon the punishment he should inflict on Willi for having entered his cave and stolen his dinner, or rather, upon the most painful

kind of death which he might give him, Willi, before adding his pelt to the catskins drying in the smoke above the cauldron. As for Willi, great was the fear that gripped his heart at the appearance of Glómr within the cave, and his own detection, but he did not let signs of his fear be seen, but continued eating the meat on the floor as if he had not seen anything, although he watched from the side of his eye to see if any means of escape should occur to him.

Glómr then raised his club and aimed a mighty blow at Willi, which struck fire from the rock of the cave, for Willi jumped around to the other side of the cauldron and avoided it. Glómr followed him around the cauldron and aimed another blow. This time he missed Willi again but his club hit the edge of the cauldron, which upset in the fire, filling the cave with dense clouds of steam and ashes.

Now Glómr could not see Willi but he rained blows here and there, wherever he thought Willi might be or where he heard him moving, and many of these blows would have felled a bull and some came very close to Willi.

At last Willi felt he could never escape fom Glómr's club and in desperation he made a leap and caught the chain of the cauldron and scrambled up the chain through smoke and soot until he had reached the shaft from the cave. Here the chain of Glómr's cauldron hung from a hook in the wall of the shaft. Glómr heard Willi climbing up the chain and with a roar of anger he started climbing up the chain too, but Willi kept ahead of him; and the end was that Glómr stuck in the shaft behind him. But Willi was able to escape through the vent, and when he got out he returned to the cave, removed the boulder at the door, and built up the fire beneath Glómr. Then he returned to the top of the shaft and flung down stones at Glómr's head, and Glómr perished miserably between the smoke of the fire and the stones cast by Willi. This deed of Willi's freed Kaney from the fear of the evil monster Glómr but cost Willi his eighth life.

Gingr and Kari his Wife

THERE was a cat called Gingr. He was a member of Willi's band and one of his most trusted henchcats. Gingr was valiant in battle and wise in Council. He had a wife called Kari. After Glómr's burning Kari had four kittens. Cats used to say that Kari was a witch. No cat knew where she came from and her looks and actions were uncanny. She had a white coat, blue eyes with a slight squint, and brown face and paws and tail. She went little amongst other cats and was silent and haughty. Gingr had met her on the shore of Kaney, and she had told him she had been shipwrecked. But other cats when speaking softly to each other would declare that she had sailed to Kaney on an eggshell, or even had blown there on a broomstick. But they did not dare to utter such thoughts within her hearing.

Now touching all that falls to be told here of the disappearance of Kari, of Gingr's search for her and of Willi's expedition to the enchanted island of Rokabarrey with Gingr in search of her, I Frukjan Frisl, who write this tale on a dark evening of winter on parchment with my quill and ink, do but relate the traditions I have heard repeated by very old and truthful cats learned in the lore of our race, and if I tell a lie a lie was told to me, for I was not present at these happenings and I did not live when it was possible to question those who had witnessed them. But here is the tale as I got it with nothing added thereto or taken from it.

The Disappearance of Kari

ONE DAY Kari and her kittens disappeared. There was great commotion amongst the cats when the news of her disappearance was learned, for many feared her as uncanny and dreaded her return in some other and more dangerous form to do them harm. Gingr who loved her and was filled with jealousy raised an outcry, searching all likely hiding-places and threatening death to any who had taken part in Kari's catnapping. It was not long before news of Kari's disappearance reached Willi and soon thereafter when he was seated in Council there was heard miaouwing at the palace door. It was Gingr seeking audience. Willi directed that Gingr should be admitted. Gingr entered looking tired and dusty.

"Who has wronged thee?" said Willi.

'My wife and kittens are stolen," said Gingr.

"Great the insult to you, King, and to your invincible followers that such an outrage should be done to any one of us." Willi agreed. Bands of cats were ordered to search the island for Kari; but no trace of her or of her kittens was found.

The Seal Garry Advises Gingr

HERE was a seal called Garry. He frequented the harbour of Kaney, in which he used to catch flounders and grey mullet. Sometimes he shared his catches with the cats when he had eaten all he could hold himself. He was friendly with the cats, who warned him of any dangers he might be in from humans, and they were well disposed towards him on account of the fish.

One day Gingr went to the shore to see if Garry had caught any fish. He found Garry sunning himself on a rock. Garry saw him coming, and spoke thus:

"Ill and weary art thou, Gingr."

"Miaou," said Gingr, "my hearth is cold and my bed is empty."

"I know," said Garry, "thy wife has left thee."

"Who told thee that?"

"There are many things," said Garry, "that

I know that cats know not, and many ways I have to learn that cats have not. I am friendly with the birds which you cats hunt."

"What news hast thou of Kari? – speak quickly."

Garry paused. Then he intoned this quatrain:

Kari hides in Rokabarrey
'Mid magic mists on silent shores
With your kittens and her kinscats –
Ne'er comes she to Kaney more.

"Who told thee that?" said Gingr.

"The blackback gulls from Hiorta and the fulmars that nest on Mikkiley," said Garry. "So it must be true."

Gingr waited no more, not even to ask if Garry had any fish, but he fared straightway to Willi and asked Willi if a viking expedition could go to Rokabarrey to rescue Kari.

"This must be discussed in Council," said Willi, and he sent word to all his leading henchcats to assemble that same evening.

Gingr Before the Council

WHEN the cats were assembled, "Let Gingr speak," said Willi, "about the affair he wishes to put before you," and Gingr stood up and spoke and told how he had learned that Kari was on Rokabarrey, and how he wished to sail with an expedition there to recover her and his kittens. When he had spoken, the cats of the Council were all silent thinking. Then a very wise and experienced cat called Sorley arose and spoke.

"We have heard, O Willi, the story of the disappearance of Gingr's wife Kari and her kittens and we agree that this is an insult to us which should be avenged. But it must be said that this expedition on which Gingr would take some of us is one of no ordinary danger and difficulty. I have heard in my youth old cats talk of Rokabarrey and one very old cat I then knew even claimed to have visited it, though we did not all believe him. But from all I heard I can tell that this Rokabarrey is no ordinary island. It is out in the open sea many miles beyond sight of Barrey or Mikkiley, and it is said that there are times when it cannot be discovered at all, for it may either lie in a magic mist which eye cannot penetrate nor ships navigate, or it may sink below the surface of the sea and be lost entirely. Further, I have heard that the island of Rokabarrey is always green, and its crops and fruit trees are always ripe, and the humans and cats that live there do not grow old and die like other cats and humans, but are always young and strong and beautiful. And in Rokabarrey there is always good hunting and good quarters, and there are none of the dangerous foes which afflict cats in other parts of the world, such as giants and catskin curers and wolves and dogs and snakes. But I have heard that no mortal cat may land there, or if he does so, then he may never return."

"Thou art old and wise, Sorley," said Willi, "or else I would never have believed what thou sayst of Rokabarrey – or rather, indeed, I do not now believe it, thinking that thou hast been deceived. But bring Garry," said Willi to some of his henchcats, "and we will question him also about this island."

So Garry was sent for and found swimming in Kaneyjarhafn and brought to Willi and the Council. Willi and Garry greeted each other with friendliness. Then Willi related to Garry what Sorley had told of Rokabarrey and asked Garry if there was truth in what Sorley had heard.

"I have not seen Rokabarrey myself," said Garry, "but I have often heard of it from my mother and from other seals and from the porpoises and dolphins that visit the shores of Kaney, and I can tell you that what Sorley has spoken is no less than the truth. I have heard indeed that Rokabarrey has other marvels, such as springs of health-giving waters that give everlasting youth to all who drink them, and abundance of cattle, sheep, fish, fowl and rare metals and jewels. Hence many humans would visit it but it is guarded by magic and enchantments."

"How could Gingr find his wife then?" said Willi.

"Not by any ordinary means," said Garry.

"But I can help him," he said. "I have here some shells of the cowry – if all who fare of this venture carry each one, thy galley can never be lost in the mist, for the cowry has virtues against the mist. And I have here a piece of yarn in which there are three knots," said Garry, "and if Gingr takes the yarn, if he is becalmed and needs a breeze to fill his sails let him untie the first knot: and if after all he needs yet a fresher breeze let him untie the second knot. But whatever happens, on no account must he untie the third knot," said Garry, "or disaster will befall him."

Willi now turned to his Council. "You have now heard Sorley and Garry tell of Rokabarrey," said Willi. "Is it your wish to fare there?" Many cats spoke then about this venture, some daringly and some cautiously. At length one of the wisest cats arose and said: "We have faced many dangers and it must never be said that we feared any venture, but this one to Rokabarrey is of no ordinary difficulty. We are willing to go but on two conditions. The first is that thou, Willi, art our leader and the second is that the government of Kaney is left in strong paws," he said; "then we shall fear nothing."

So it was agreed. Willi was to captain the expedition and his son Will Willisson would rule Kaney with a Council of wise cats until Willi and Gingr and their henchcats returned with Kari.

Sailing to Rokabarrey

Willi Sails for Rokabarrey

So WILLI and his cats went where their galley *Eelnose* was lying pulled up on the shore, and they launched her. Then they turned her bow to the sea and her stern to the shore and they hoosted her towering, speckled sails to her tall, well-tried masts so that neither mast was bent nor sail was torn, and they put out upon the white-capped windswept ocean where the great fishes feed upon the small and the small do the best they can for themselves; the crooked grey whelks of the deep were striking against the galley's keel as she lay in the wave-troughs and the tops of the galley's masts were lost in the clouds when she rose on wave-crests; her helmscat steered her while her lookout guided her; each bound rope in her was loosened and each loose rope in her was tied. And in this fashion Willi and his cats sailed out into the mighty Minch with favouring breezes until they passed through the rocks and islands of Barreyjarsund into the

open Atlantic. And when they had sailed so far that the tops of the hills of Vist and Barrey were sinking into the eastern skyline, a calm came on them. And when they were becalmed Gingr asked Willi to loosen the first knot in the yarn that Garry had given them, and Willi did so, and a soft breeze came up out of the southeast and took them out of sight of land. This fell away again and calm came on them once more, and a thick mist. The mist was moving with the galley, shrouding them so that they did not know where they were. Then Willi told each cat to lay a hold of one of the cowries they had, and the mist parted before them on their course and they rowed out of the magic mist. Then Willi untied the second knot in the yarn and a good fresh breeze sprang up behind them. And as they sped before the breeze they beheld far to the west the low-lying hills of a well-favoured island, that is, Rokabarrey. And when they had approached so near that they could see the green woods and white sands and the habitations of the Island, the breeze again fell away and they were again becalmed. Willi called on them to row, but his cats were weary. "Open the third knot," called Gingr, "no harm can befall us now we are so near." Willi untied it. No sooner had he done so than a furious mighty blast came up out of the south-east with huge waves, hailstones, thunder and lightning. *Eelnose* was caught up by the waves and wind and cast in an instant upon the rocks of the shore of Rokabarrey, and was broken into fragments, and Willi and Gingr and their cats were cast into the breakers and climbed ashore with great difficulty after nearly drowning.

Thus they reached Rokabarrey, where Gingr found Kari and her kittens and her kinsfolk, and lived with them there ever afterwards. As for Willi and his henchcats, they were not ever beheld of humans or of cats again, for, as it is said, it is possible for mortal cats to land on Rokabarrey if they can find it but none has ever left it to return to the land of mortals. And it is related to this day that Willi and his henchcats are living in Rokabarrey in the bloom of everlasting youth and vigour. No cat has seen them there but this tale is told by seals and gulls and fulmars and who shall doubt it, knowing all the wonders Rokabarrey holds, and which I have already related? This is the tale of Willi as it has been told to me, and as it is told by the descendants of Willi who rule over Kaney to this day, and I have put it down on parchment so that the fame of Will and his doings may be remembered ever after.

THE END

Wicked William and Mr. Smith
at the kitchen door, Nordhrvagr, Barrey

John Lorne Campbell

John Lorne Campbell was born in Edinburgh on 1 October 1906 and an interest in Gaelic was nurtured through his upbringing in Argyll on the family lands of the Campbells of Inverneil and Taynish. After school in Edinburgh and at Rugby, he studied Rural Economy at St John's College, Oxford, and studied Scottish Gaelic with Professor John Fraser, Professor of Celtic in Oxford, who also encouraged him in his research which bore fruit in the ground-breaking *Highland Songs of the Forty-Five* (1933). This set a pattern with scrupulous editing and scholarship and a robust setting straight the record for Highland and Hebridean history which was to mark his career of research and publication in Celtic Studies.

John Lorne Campbell moved to Barra in August 1933 and began the recording of the everyday language of the community and, with the latest mechanical recording equipment, pioneered live-recording in the field. He met the American musician, Margaret Fay Shaw, in Lochboisdale, South Uist (the same setting for *WikkedWillisSaga*), and they were married in Glasgow in May 1935. Together they bought the Island of Canna in 1938 and set up a hospitable house which drew to it their Hebridean friends and a worldwide following over more than half a century. Together John and Margaret built up an archive of Gaelic song and story, a library for Scottish and Celtic Studies and a unique record of farming and entomology in the islands. His intense scientific study of flora and fauna included, naturally for him, the close observation of the domesticated animals of Canna and those who knew John and Margaret remember their fondness and respect for cats and the eponymous hero, 'Wicked Willie'.

His island property, successfully farmed in interests of conservation, together with his and Margaret's extensive collections of field recordings, writings and correspondence, were donated to the National Trust for Scotland in 1981 to form a resource in the public domain for the continuing study of the language, culture and environment of the Highlands and Islands. His sound recordings now form the foundation of the *Tobar an Dualchais/Kist o Riches* digital resource.

John Lorne Campbell's publication of the Gaelic record was designed to raise awareness of its extraordinary richness and integrity, and to set new editorial standards, for example, as in the three volumes of *Hebridean Folksongs* (1969-1981, co-authored with Francis Collinson) and his 'Six Stories' or *Sia Sgialachdan* (1939) from reciters in South Uist and Barra. This latter work raised the interest of the Irish Folklore Commission in the strength of the oral tradition of the Hebrides and led ultimately to the establishment of the School of Scottish Studies in the University of Edinburgh in 1951. In the early 1930s, he had looked beyond this Gaelic community to the diaspora, and he visited Canada and the descendants of emigrants of 1790-1835 in Nova Scotia to discover the extent to which they had sustained their culture. His recordings were published in *Songs Remembered in Exile* (1990), showing that what had been lost from the song tradition of the Highlands and Hebrides through swingeing clearance and emigration formed part of a living repertory in the New World. At home, his fieldwork continued with the recording of, among others, the vast personal repertoire of Angus MacLellan of South Uist (see *Tales from South Uist*, 1961) and the publication of the storyteller's life history in *The Furrow Behind Me* (1962) and *Saoghal an Treobhaiche* (1972). This was matched by major studies of earlier remarkable collectors from the Celticist, Edward Lhuyd (1660-1709), to Fr Allan McDonald of Eriskay (1859-1905) whose career and collections he published in a biography (1954), *Gaelic Words and Expressions from South Uist and Eriskay* (1958) and *Bàrdachd Mhgr Ailein: the Gaelic Poems of Fr Allan McDonald* (1965).

John Lorne Campbell maintained a steady flow of scholarly articles across disciplines in the humanities and sciences, his published research in journals such as *Scottish Gaelic Studies* and *The Innes Review* still providing a staple and benchmarks for Celtic Studies. His collections of *Macrolepidoptera Cannae* and field records of scientific observation add specialist dimensions to his farming operations, also scientifically observed and scrupulously recorded. Much of this is brought into sharp focus for posterity in his *Canna. The Story of a Hebridean Island* (1984). John Lorne Campbell died near Fiesole in Italy on 25 April 1996 and his mortal remains were reinterred in Canna in 2006.

Hugh Cheape
Sabhal Mòr Ostaig
An Giblean 2015